T0197536

MaryEllen IS Stuck!!!!

MaryEllen Perlini
Illustrated by: Gail Jacalan

To order additional copies of this book, contact:
Xlibris
844-714-8691
www.Xlibris.com
Orders@Xlibris.com

ISBN: Softcover   978-1-6698-5390-9
         Hardcover   978-1-6698-5392-3
         EBook   978-1-6698-5391-6

Print information available on the last page

Rev. date: 11/21/2022

This book is dedicated to my fabulous family and fantastic friends whom I love, love, love; they continuously encourage, inspire, and guide me!!!

1

MaryEllen is stuck. She is stuck, stuck, stuck!!!

When she is stuck, she shops. She shops, shops, shops!!!

She shops for shoes.

She shops for sweaters.

She shops for pants.

She shops for coats.

MaryEllen does not have the money to shop for shoes, sweaters, pants, and coats because she is broke. She is broke, broke, broke, just like her peasant, Italian relatives!!!

The more she shops, the less money she has. Then MaryEllen loses confidence in her life and has no enthusiasm.

During the pandemic, MaryEllen shopped online because the local stores were closed. They were closed, closed, closed!!! MaryEllen, along with her family and friends, enjoy other activities besides shopping such as yoga, dancing, movies, concerts, and going out for coffee and nachos.

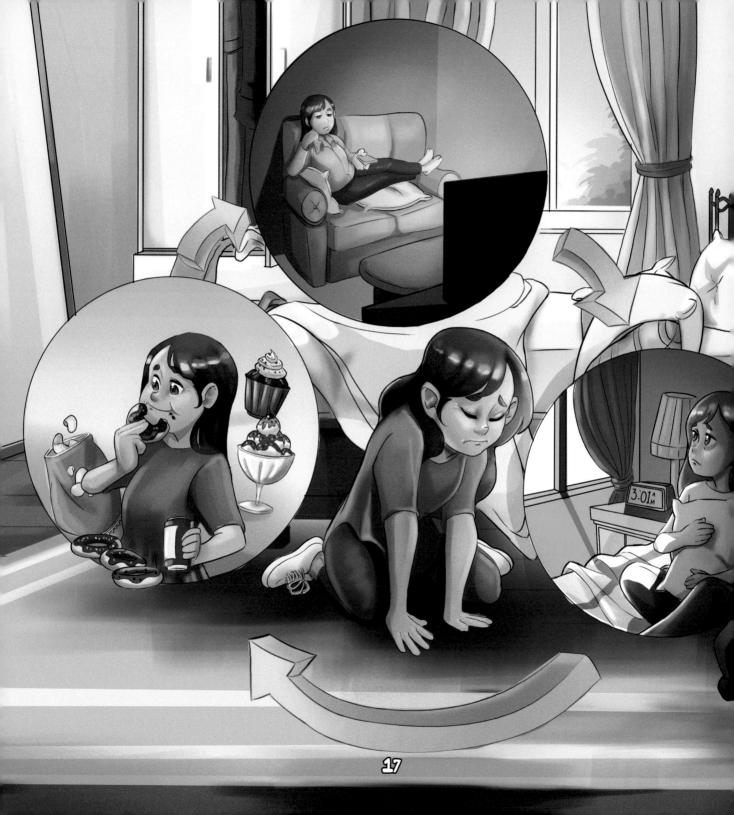

Since it was the pandemic, there was
nothing happening in the community and
they certainly could not go out for coffee
and nachos. MaryEllen is definitely stuck
in unfamiliar territory!!!

She lacks confidence and enthusiasm.

One day, MaryEllen's hairdresser, Julie, calls to change her hair appointment. MaryEllen says yes. She says yes, yes, yes!!!

When she parks her car for her hair appointment, MaryEllen notices a Parking Attendant. She notices that he is busy. He is busy, busy, busy!!! He is also so confident and enthusiastic. Up and down, up, and down, up, and down he walks. He walks up and down the entire parking lot with his bright, special vest and thick, brown clipboard.
He has a spring in his step.

That day, MaryEllen is inspired. She is inspired, inspired, inspired!!! MaryEllen remembers having a bright, special vest and a thick, brown clipboard like the Parking Attendant.

After her hair appointment, MaryEllen puts on her bright, special vest and grabs the thick, brown clipboard like the Parking Attendant, and she feels confident and enthusiastic. Her confidence and enthusiasm grows, and grows, and grows!!!

She goes to work the next day with such a spring in her step and shows everyone who is interested her bright, special vest and thick, brown clipboard.

MaryEllen spreads her confidence and enthusiasm to people she encounters.

Guess what happens?

The people who try on her bright, special, vest and carry her thick, brown clipboard feel confident and enthusiastic too!!!

The good news of this confidence and enthusiasm spreads.

It spreads, spreads, spreads all the way to Italy!!!

Yes, Italy, where MaryEllen's family originated!!!

Many people are asking MaryEllen to share her story, bright, special vest, and thick, brown clipboard because they want to gain confidence and enthusiasm too.

MaryEllen is no longer stuck. She is busy, busy, busy, has a spring in her step and she does not have time to shop as much.

THE END

Printed in the United States
by Baker & Taylor Publisher Services